THE PIXIKINS

THE PIXIKINS

Juliet Russell-Roberts

Illustrated by
Pauline Callais

ISBN: 978-1-9999389-0-1

Digital ISBN: 978-1-9999389-1-8

www.julietrussellroberts.com

To Anita

I

There are worlds upon worlds upon worlds, all superimposed on top of one another, existing at one and the same time. The pixikins travel between them by means of a protective bubble.

'Have you ever seen a pixikin?' said the tortoise. 'They are easily recognisable by their balls of fluffy yellow hair and blue Lycra jumpsuits.'

And those are not the only things that they are recognisable for, for the pixikins are the smallest of the small. Take the size of a thimble and then halve it, and then – go on – halve it again. But what they lack for in size, they more than make up for in spirit, for the pixikins have the furthest reaching vision of all the species. The pixikins can see places that you and I – fellow humans – could only ever have dreamt about. Until now, that is. Until a little girl named Tala accidentally trod upon a banana skin and slipped, quite suddenly, into another dimension.

'Wah, wah, wah,' wailed Tala, as she sat on the ground rubbing her eyes. 'Wah, wah, wah.'

Tala's hands were all grazed from the fall, but

that was not really why she was crying. It was
just an excuse to cry. The tears had been – if you
will – brewing all day. The fights with her family.
Being ignored. Being unloved. Being told that she
was useless and pathetic all the time. It was all too
much for a little girl, even a strong little girl like
Tala, and so she had sought refuge in the woods.
She had packed a little bag and run away. She did
not have anywhere to go, nor did she have anyone
to go to, but just the peace and quiet of being on
her own was enough to spur her on. And now look
at her. Here she was in a heap on the floor, her
little red dress muddy and torn. It really was a sorry
sight, a sorry life, and so what else was there to do

but cry?

Her sobbing got louder and louder by the second: so loud, in fact, that Rollo could scarcely concentrate on what he was doing.

'What is that awful racket?' he said out loud to himself, as he put down his paintbrush and peeped his head around the side of the tree.

'Oh my,' he gasped, for it was indeed a sorry sight: a fair damsel in distress.

What was she doing out on her own in the middle of the woods? he wondered, as he stepped a little closer to her, and then a little closer still, for Rollo knew well by now that, whilst he can see into the human realm, the human realm cannot see or hear him.

'You see,' said the tortoise, 'Rollo is a pixikin, and everyone knows that a pixikin is vibrating at a different level to a human being, just as an angel is vibrating at a different level to a fairy, and so on and so forth. It is perfectly simple, really.'

Rollo stopped short directly in front of Tala.

'Do not worry little girl,' he said out loud, 'for I have a feeling that everything is going to be just fine.'

But, very much to his surprise, she stopped crying and started scanning the ground in front of her with her eyes.

'Who said that?' she said.

'Said what?' he replied.

'That!' she exclaimed.

And with that, Rollo boldly stepped forward and raised his arms up into the air.

'Ta da!'

II

By now, Rollo was comfortably seated in the palm of Tala's left hand, which was held up towards her face, for they had much that they needed to discuss. Both were as excited as the other by what had come to pass. Rollo had been around humans all his life, but this was the first time that he had actually had a two-way conversation with one of them. Tala had always known – felt inside – that there was more to life than the narrow confines of the world in which she had hitherto been living, but this was the first time that she had proof of it.

'The trouble with you humans,' Rollo said, 'is that you do not seem to notice directly what is in front of you.'

'Well, if you were not so little...' Tala retorted indignantly. But then she thought of the hordes of people that she saw moving along the streets like cattle, knocking into one another as if the other were not even there, as if they were the only thing that mattered.

'You are so caught up in your make-believe worlds – getting from A to B,' Rollo continued, 'that you do not have time and space for anything else. You take the little things – like what house you live in, or what car you drive – so seriously, that you do not have time for the things that really matter.'

'Like, what is my purpose? Why am I here?' Tala said. 'Do you mean that sort of thing?'

'Yes, Tala, exactly so,' Rollo replied. 'And those questions are not easy to answer – not even for a pixikin,' he went on. 'But we must always follow our hearts. Then we can never go wrong. That is how us pixikins live our lives.'

'You mean,' Tala said with widening eyes, 'you do not tell each other what to do?'

'No, Tala,' Rollo laughed. 'We find our answers within.'

And as Tala was musing on what it would be like to follow her heart rather than her orders, they heard the sound of voices – human voices – approaching.

'Uh-oh,' Tala said, 'we must hide. Quick!'

And with that Rollo laughed again.

'Oh, don't you worry about me. I could be doing backflips,' he said, as he did a backflip, 'and somersaults,' he added, as he did a somersault in the air, 'and shouting out: "Cooey"!' he shouted out, 'and still they would not see me.'

'But...'

And just then, they – the strangers – appeared. They were not two feet away. Tala froze to the spot, her mind racing – at least a thousand thoughts a second. *What shall I say? What will they say? I will have to lie and say my mother is here with me. What if they are nasty and try to kidnap me? What if they try to help me and take me back home? Urghh, home. What if they heard me talking? What if...? What if...? What if...?* But her concerns were all in vain, for the strangers carried on straight past her. She looked at Rollo and Rollo looked at her.

'Hey!' Tala shouted, in spite of herself, but nothing. She ran towards them, and then in front of them, beating her hands on her chest like a gorilla, but still, absolutely nothing.

You see, Tala had entered into the realm of the pixikins. She was now vibrating at their level, and this was something that had never been done before. She was vibrating at too high a frequency now for mere earthly eyes to see. But the world still looked the same, was the same: nothing had changed, it was just that Tala could see more. As well as seeing what humans could see, she could see what the pixikins could see. She looked all around her and noticed that the colours of the trees, the earth, the sky, were so much sharper than she had realised. There was a natural beauty in everything that she saw. Instead of a tree just being a tree, it was a living entity, just as she was. And as she looked a little closer at a tree, she noticed several little pixikins wedged into the bark, all looking out at her in awe.

'You see,' said the tortoise, 'the layers of the universe exist on top of one another. The denser the layer, the less you can see, and the humans are the densest of the lot. The higher – or more subtle – the layer, the more you can see.'

The tortoise stopped for a sip of herbal tea, and then continued:

'Imagine a staircase leading up to the sky,' he said. 'With each step up, you can see back down, but you can never see ahead. Not unless you are a pixikin, that is. A pixikin has a free pass to travel between all the layers of the universe, for a pixikin is in a dimension all of its own. A pixikin is the all-seeing, all-knowing mediator between the realms, if you will. You do not need to be a rocket scientist to understand what I am telling you.'

Tala and Rollo looked at each other again, and then Rollo did a humble bow.

'At your service, Ma'am,' he said.

'Oh please,' Tala laughed. 'Do stop being so silly. But I must say, I am rather curious. What on earth is going on? Is this all some big dream, I wonder? And where have all your little friends gone? I saw them just now.'

She went towards the tree and peered more closely at it.

'It is no good hiding,' she said. 'I know that you are there.'

But this elicited little response.

'I shall count to ten,' she continued, 'and if you have not shown yourselves by then, why, I shall simply have to come and get you myself. One, two, three, four, five...'

And just then she saw a little foot sticking out of the tree. She seized the moment and grabbed ahold of it between her forefinger and thumb, and then pulled a pixikin straight up and out into the air, his little legs flailing.

'Uh-ahh,' he pronounced, somewhat clumsily, as his little wizard hat fell off and tumbled to the floor.

Tala held him at eye level for a moment and then looked him up and down. Yes, he was definitely a pixikin. He had the same characteristic enormous ball of fluffy yellow hair and rather silly blue Lycra jumpsuit on. But he was older than Rollo. You could see it in the lines of wisdom on his face.

'Well,' she said.

The pixikin took a moment to gather his composure before looking Tala directly in the eye.

'I, Cornucopious the 10th,' he said, as he did an upside-down bow, 'am also at your service.'

III

It turns out that Cornucopious was the oldest, wisest pixikin of the lot – the wizard amongst them, if you will. He was nearing his one thousandth year, and yet even in his long reign of pixikinhood, he had never encountered a situation like this before. Ordinarily, human beings simply could not see or hear or even begin to fathom what a pixikin might be. The lucky few could sometimes catch glimpses of other dimensions, but only those dimensions a little closer to their own. What Tala appeared to have done was to have slipped right off the bottom step of the ladder, if you will, and to have somehow landed on the top step, and then out into no man's land: the all-seeing, all-knowing realm of the pixikins.

But how and why had this come to pass?

'Come to think of it,' Tala said, 'as I tripped on that banana skin, I did feel something rather strange; it was almost like an electric shock.'

'Go on,' Cornucopious gently encouraged.

'Yes,' she said, 'like a spark of energy. I was falling, and yet somehow, I wasn't falling at all. I was effortlessly floating, as if everything were happening in slow motion, as if there were hands holding me up.'

'Ah-hah,' said Cornucopious, 'you were being guided as you crossed the realms – passed between them, if you will.'

'And I must say,' Tala said, as she looked up at the sky dreamily, 'it was rather a nice feeling. A little like bliss, I suppose.'

She paused, before continuing:

'But in a moment that magical feeling was gone, and I landed with a thud on the ground. See.'

She held her grazed hands out for Cornucopious to see.

'And that is when I started to cry,' she said.

CHAPTER III

'For a minute, I felt that life can be beautiful, but then I came crashing back down to reality, and I remembered that the world is a mean and cruel place.'

'But Tala, do you not see?' Cornucopious replied. 'What you have done is nothing short of a miracle. A wise old man once told me that this would happen one day, but I was beginning to doubt if I would see it in my lifetime.'

'That what would happen?' Tala asked.

'That a very special little girl would come and change the world,' Cornucopious replied, as he looked at Tala directly in the eyes.

'Oh please,' Tala laughed, 'I am only a useless little girl. What difference could I possibly make?'

'You see,' said the tortoise, 'that is what Tala had been led to believe all her life – that she was nothing – and it can take a little time sometimes to right the wrongs of our past. The task now was to help her to see that, in actual fact, she was decidedly more than nothing, and to help her become the little girl that she was destined to become.'

IV

The pixikins welcomed Tala as one of their own. They adored her, and, most importantly, they listened to what she had to say. When Tala asked them questions, they told her truthful answers – none of that fobbing off that she was used to, none of that assuming that she would not understand the truth because she was a little girl – and this was an altogether alien experience for Tala. If all these pixikins were being so nice to her, perhaps she was not so bad after all, or perhaps she was merely a pixikin born in a human body. Yes, she rather liked that theory, far-fetched though it may sound. But the truth is, Tala was different to the masses. She had tried her hardest to fit in, to be a good girl, to do her homework, to do the things that all her friends enjoyed, but she was always yearning for more. Life, as she had known it, had always seemed somewhat futile.

As a very small child she had felt a connection to something much vaster. She had seen and heard things that other people could not see and hear. She had known things without knowing why she knew them, but little by little she had been worn down, told that she was making it all up, told that she was nothing short of crazy. And so she had trained herself not to believe in all the wondrous things that she had believed in; she had shut the joy out of her life for fear of reprimand and disapproval. She had become – on the surface – just like everyone else, but she had been living a lie.

Tala was eight years old now, a pivotal age in her life, where she could well have continued on down the path to obscurity, but this lucky act of fate – or opportune positioning of a banana skin, or whatever you like to call it – had given her the wake-up call that she so needed to turn her life around. And in this Tala had been luckier than most, for once we set off down the wrong path, it is so often a cycle that continues week upon week, and year upon year until, before we know it, life has somehow passed us by. But of course, Tala had taken rather a large jump in one fell swoop, and so, naturally, she needed a little time to acclimatise, to find her feet, if you will, and so the pixikins let her be. By day, she would roam about, freely marvelling in all that was around her, and by night, hundreds of pixikins would huddle up against her – keeping her warm with their body heat.

One day, Tala was out walking in the woods by

herself, and she saw the most beautiful butterfly. She followed it – meandering through the trees – until it perched on a little branch not two feet away.

'Oh my,' she said, 'you are a handsome fellow.' But as she got a little closer still, she saw that it was not a butterfly at all. It had little legs and little arms. Why, it was a miniature human, but with beautiful wings. And just at that moment, it took off again.

'Hey!' Tala shouted out. 'Come back here. I won't hurt you!' But it was no use. The human-like butterfly either did not want to or could not hear her.

Of course, back home, if something like that had happened, she would have shrugged her shoulders and told herself that she was making it up, but little by little, a life with the pixikins was giving her the courage to speak up.

'Rollo, Rollo!' she shouted out loud, as she ran back towards the pixikin dwellings. 'You'll never guess what I saw?'

'A flying saucer?' he asked, with a mischievous twinkle in his eye, as she found him in his usual position, hard at work – doing goodness only knows what – within a tree hollow.

'No, silly,' she laughed. 'A mini human with wings.'

'Ah,' he said, becoming quite serious. 'Now that must have been a resident from the Fairy Kingdom. Yes, they rather like to spend time in nature.'

'The Fairy Kingdom?' Tala asked, incredulous. 'But I thought that they were make-believe.'

'In much the same way that a pixikin is make-believe, do you mean?' he replied, as he pinched her skin, as if waking her up from a dream.

'Ahhh,' she laughed, 'you beastly monster!' And how they chuckled together.

'But why wouldn't that fairy talk to me?' Tala continued.

'For the very same reason that human beings no longer see you, Tala,' Rollo replied, 'for you are vibrating too highly for even a fairy's eyes.'

'But... I only wanted to play,' Tala said, a little dejectedly, and at this Rollo stopped what he was doing and spent the rest of the afternoon playing hopscotch and tiddlywinks and skipping ropes, until he was quite worn out.

Another day, she saw what, at first sight, she thought were two human beings, but as they drew closer, she realised that one of them had the most beautiful wings. She did her usual:

'Hey!'

But nothing. And so she just stood back and

observed, marvelling in all that was around her.

And when she saw a man being followed by a tiger, she went to alert him:

'Hey, you, watch out!'

But the man carried on oblivious. The tiger carried on, oblivious, and it certainly did not look like it was out to harm the man. Little by little, Tala came to expect the unexpected and not to question it, to accept life as it was and not to meddle in it, and this continued day upon day and night upon night, until one morning Tala saw some young girls – about her age – playing at the edge of the forest. They were laughing and having fun, and Tala so longed to laugh and have fun with them, but they simply could not see or hear her. Tala sat down on the ground – not two feet away from them – with her head in her hands, and as if by magic, Rollo appeared.

'Boo,' he said, as he peeked his little head up from behind a branch, but Tala scarcely paid any attention to him.

'I see you have a little dose of the blues,' he added, but Tala merely shrugged her shoulders.

'Come now,' he went on, 'I think the time has come for you to talk with Cornucopious again.'

V

Rollo led Tala on a long journey through the forest, so far that her little feet were beginning to ache.

'Are we nearly there?' she asked, somewhat brattishly.

'Oh just another few miles to go,' Rollo replied.

'A few miles?' she queried. 'Well I, for one, simply do not see how an old pixikin like Cornucopious could travel this far every day.'

'Well, us pixikins have other means of travelling than by foot,' he replied.

'Well, I certainly have not seen any methods of transport since I have been here, and believe you me, I have been looking around,' Tala retorted. 'Nope. No bicycles. No cars. No boats. No buses. No trains. No roller skates. No nothing. You might as well be living in the Dark Ages,' she added, for Tala was feeling a little crotchety by now.

Rollo did not react; instead he allowed a moment of silence before continuing.

'Unfortunately, our method of transportation is – now, how shall we say it – a little too small for you. That is why we have been taking you places by foot. But ordinarily we travel through the air.'

'Through the air?' Tala queried. 'Well, I have not seen any aeroplanes either on my travels, or hang-gliders, or paragliders, or...'

But just then she stopped, for she had a fleeting memory of seeing some bubbles one day, way up high in the sky. She turned to look at Rollo, and Rollo nodded his head in agreement.

'Yes, Tala,' he said. 'That is how we travel.'

'How?' Tala said, with widening eyes, for she had not actually said anything. But no sooner had she spoken, than she saw, in her mind's eye, a series of bubbles with one pixikin in each, all swishing their legs back and forth as the bubbles moved forwards.

'What was that?' she said.

'You asked,' Rollo said, 'and so I showed you. Sometimes images are so much easier than words, don't you think?'

And at this, Tala was a little taken aback.

'You mean...' she said, and before she could say the words she was thinking, he replied.

'Yes.'

'Stop doing that,' she said.

'Well, you asked,' he replied, for indeed it turns out that Rollo could both see what Tala could see, in her mind's eye, and, indeed, hear what she was thinking, and so there really was no need for actual conversation.

Tala went into a huff, and as she did, she said in her head: *I'll show you. Know what I am thinking indeed. Well, how about this? You look like a banana.* And no sooner had she said it, she sensed the words, 'Ooh, lucky me. I just love bananas,' and she looked back at Rollo and he smiled.

You see, it was not just Rollo who could do it, for Tala too was vibrating at his level, and so Tala too could do the things that he could do. And so the rest of the journey was spent in this way: sending each other thoughts, images – you name it. And that got Tala thinking of all those nasty thoughts that she had had about other people in the past, and she somehow wished that she could take them back, for perhaps just a nasty thought has the power to hurt somebody. And so she vowed to keep herself – or rather her judgements – in check from that day forth. We are all unique after all. Who was she to say that one person is better than the next?

At last, they arrived at a clearing, and Cornucopious was standing all by himself – resplendent in his wizard clothes – in the very centre of it.

'Cornucopious!' Tala shrieked, as she ran towards him, quite forgetting how tired she was.

She lay down on the muddy floor so that her face was parallel to his, and then proceeded to tell him about all the wondrous things that she had seen since seeing him last. He listened attentively, smiling, laughing, joking, and only when she had finished, did he become quite serious, and said:

'Now, I gather you have been shown our method of transport.'

'Oh, you are a mind-reader too are you?' she asked, but she did not even need him to answer that one, because she already knew what was coming next.

'You have been working all this time on a bubble that is large enough and strong enough to carry me,' she said. 'And now that the work is complete, well, it is time for me to move on.'

And at this she looked down at the ground.

'You want to get rid of me,' she said.

'No, no, dear girl, we'd love for you to stay, but the universe has other plans in store for you, I am afraid,' he replied.

Tala's eyes remained fixed on the ground.

'And besides,' he went on, 'you are a human. You need interaction with others. You would not be satisfied if you could never speak to your own kind again.'

'That is not true,' she said, but she knew as she said it, that it was, in fact, true. Just that very morning she had come to know it for herself.

She admitted defeat.

'What is it that you would have me do?' she asked.

'Well,' he said, 'you came shooting up here rather quickly. Now, what we propose, is to send you back down again, but not like the speed of lightning. Slower than that. Send you down in stages so that you may integrate everything that you saw and yet could not quite comprehend on your way up. Do you follow?'

'I think so,' Tala replied. 'And then what?' she went on. 'Life carries on as normal?'

'No Tala, you have changed, you can never go back to that little girl that you were when you packed your little bundle of things and fled. You will see the world through a different lens. You will see the truth and you can spread the truth, and you can help many on their path.'

Tala stood there motionless, and it was about that moment, that she noticed that she was surrounded by pixikins. Yes, they had travelled far and wide to see her off, to catch one last glimpse – in their dimension, that is – of the prodigal child.

'It is a great honour that has been bestowed upon you, Tala,' Cornucopious went on. 'We have tried to help the human race, but in most cases they are too far gone to receive our guidance. You, Tala, you are one of them, and you can help them more than we ever could.'

Tala felt a little silly and woefully unprepared. She could not believe that this was her task, for all her life she had been led to believe that she was nothing, a mere irritation to be brushed aside, and so she had learnt ways to hide away in the corner. And now, here she was in the centre of the crowd being told that she had great work to achieve. She

could not, would not believe it. She wanted to
close her eyes and go to sleep, or to lock herself in
a little room and play games all day, but apparently
the universe had bigger plans in store for her. She
knew that she could not shirk her responsibilities in
life, and so, after much deliberation, she stepped
forward.

'I am not quite sure that I am what you say I
am,' she said, 'but I do not wish to let anyone
down, and I am honoured to have made your
acquaintance, and so I will do whatever I can.'

'And with that,' said the tortoise, 'Tala had taken
one major step forwards towards the fulfilment
of her destiny. And although she could not see
it now, her life thus far had prepared her for the
challenges that would follow, for everything in this
life – whether good or bad – has a wider purpose
in the grand scheme of things. Tala's time alone
had taught her to be unusually independent for a
girl of eight. The rows at home had taught her to
be strong, and to stand up for what she believed
in. The lack of meaning in her life had forced her to
seek out what she had now found. I trust you get
my gist by now.'

VI

There was a veritable flurry of activity in the hours that followed – preparing Tala for her great departure. The truth is, this had never been done before, and so it took a little time to oil the wheels, if you will. It was agreed that Rollo would be Tala's faithful companion through the realms. Her guide. To show her what was what, and who was who. But first things first. They had to test the bubble. Rollo did a demonstration. He withdrew a tube of bubble liquid from his pocket – you know the type – and then lifted out the bubble stick. He blew and he blew and he blew, and when the bubble was just about the size of him, he upped and jumped in through the bubble blower and right into the bubble itself. The bubble sealed around him with the bubble stick enclosed.

'Now you see me,' he said, as he floated around in the air, doing rather showy-offy spin turns.

'And now you don't,' he added, as he disappeared goodness only knows where.

'Now you see me!' he shouted out, as he reappeared.

'And now you don't,' he added, as he evaporated into nothingness.

'Now you see me,' he said one more time, as he materialised not two feet in front of Tala's eyes. 'And...'

Only this time he was cut short by Cornucopious.

'Come now Rollo, this is not a magic show,' he said, adding, 'I trust that I can count on you to behave yourself as you make your way through the realms, to set a good example to Tala?'

'Oh yes,' Rollo replied, as he leapt up and out of the bubble like the speed of light, and landed in an exaggeratedly studious position on the ground.

'Hmm,' Cornucopious muttered in disbelief, as he scratched his chin, before turning to Tala. 'Now Tala, it is your turn.'

Tala took a little gulp and then stepped to the fore.

'We are ready,' he shouted, and at this, a little drum roll sounded, and a group of pixikins emerged carrying a much larger tube of bubble liquid above their heads.

They stopped short in front of Tala, and Tala knelt down as they held the tube up for her. She took it in her hands.

'I have been working on this for many years, Tala,' Cornucopious said. 'At times, I wanted to throw in the towel. I felt like I was getting nowhere. At other times, I questioned the validity of what I was doing. "What use is a bubble tube fit for a human, when there are no humans in the realm of the pixikins?" I questioned. But something compelled me to keep moving forward. And that was faith. I tell you this now, because there may be times when you want to throw in the towel, when you may question the purpose of what you are doing, but you must learn – as I too have learnt, as we pixikins all have learnt – to trust in the process. Do you follow?'

'I think so,' Tala said, rather shyly.

'Now, what say we give it a go?' he said, and with that Tala lifted the lid and produced a bubble stick.

She held it out in front of her mouth, and then, with a reassuring nod from Cornucopious, gently blew into it. A bubble emerged, and she blew and she blew, just a little at a time, and with each blow the bubble got a little bigger. It was scarcely possible. It just kept on growing. Bigger and bigger and bigger. The end was nearly in sight. The bubble was nearly big enough, and Tala blew with all her might. And all of a sudden it burst.

'Oh bother!' she exclaimed, but the pixikins

were in no hurry.

'What were you thinking about when it burst?' Cornucopious asked, and Tala was a little embarrassed to tell the truth, but she figured that Cornucopious would already know the truth anyway.

'Well,' she said, 'since you asked, I was thinking how clever I was to have managed first time, and then I got scared, and felt that I had to do it, to prove that I was special.'

'Ah yes,' he said, 'you became attached to the outcome, rather than the process.'

'I suppose so,' Tala said, quietly.

'What say we try it again, and do not worry, we have all the time in the world,' he said.

And Tala did try it again – not once, not twice, not thrice, but sixteen times – and, indeed, it was when she herself was just about to throw in the towel, that it suddenly all clicked into place.

Everything is as it is meant to be, she reflected, *if this bubble bursts, it bursts. It means I am not ready for it not to burst. I am learning from this.* And that, of course, is when it did not burst. Tala was beginning to understand. She held the stick out in front of her, just as Rollo had done, and then jumped up into the air – not questioning how

or why or if it would work – and she felt a sort of inward suction from the bubble as she slipped right in.

Rollo hopped back into a bubble beside her, and from this standpoint he showed her all the tricks of the trade. It was perfectly simple really. To move at walking pace, you walk. To move faster, you swish your arms and legs back and forth, and to move at rocket pace, why, you point your feet and stretch your arms up in front – superman style. To come out, you simply do a star jump, and the moment your feet and hands all touch the side of the bubble, the bubble bursts. It was actually rather fun.

There was one move, however, that Rollo saved until last, for once Tala took this move, there would be no turning back. No one needed to say it. Once Tala left the realm of the pixikins, she would not be going back, and so when her training was nearly complete she instinctively said her farewells to her dear little friends with tears in her eyes. She picked Cornucopious clean up off the ground.

'Can I not take you with me, in my pocket?' she asked, and how he laughed, but his laughter too, was tinted with sadness, and a little tear came out of his eye.

'An old pixikin like me?' he said. 'Oh you'd soon get bored of me. Now you run along dear girl, and remember: even if you cannot see us, we are always with you. You can always call upon us for help.'

And with that, Tala upped and inned to a bubble. Rollo followed suit. He spun around like a spinning top. Tala did the same. And – poof – they were gone.

VII

They spun out into the Milky Way. Tala saw the stars, the moon, and the earth. She held her arms out in front of her and flew all around them, like the speed of light, with Rollo, ever by her side. No words were needed to explain the inexplicable. This was the universe in all its glory. Tala had seen it so many times as a small child, peering out through her bedroom window, wondering what it all meant. And now, here she was in the thick of it, and it all made perfect sense. She was a part of it, after all, and it was a part of her.

Round and round and round they flew. Tala was totally absorbed in the moment, so much so, that she did not, at first, notice that Rollo was trying to catch her attention. He sped up and halted directly in front of her, and then he did a little jig. And when, and only when, he had her attention, he nodded. Tala understood that it was time to cut back into wherever it was that they were going next. They said a simultaneous mental count of three, and then they spun, and as they were spinning, they spun back into the exact same spot that they had left.

'Three, two, one,' Rollo said, and they did a star

jump each, and landed on the ground side-by-side.

Tala lay back on the ground, and remained there motionless. It was as if she were taking everything in that she had just seen, integrating it into her very being. Rollo sat there, ever present, by her side, until she was quite ready, and then he gently brought her back.

'Tala, Tala,' he softly spoke, and little by little she gathered her composure and sat upright.

'Well, I must say,' she said, her eyes lit up with all that she had just seen, 'whatever are we doing back here?'

'We always leave and return to the same spot, Tala,' Rollo replied, and then Tala got it.

On the surface this may look like where they had just been, but they were now inside another layer, if you will, a different rung on the ladder.

'So the pixikins are all here, right now, only I cannot see them,' Tala said, with a hint of sadness in her voice.

'That's right,' Rollo said, 'but what say we go and find out what you can see?'

'Okay,' Tala said. 'Fare thee well Cornucopious, until we meet again,' she added as they set off through the forest.

Many things were exactly as they had been

before. She saw a little winged fairy, and yet still she could not speak to her. She saw some animals, but they were not interested either, and so on they went on their merry way.

After trudging around the forest for what seemed like an age, Tala stopped still.

'Well, this is a barrel of laughs,' she said, with a hint of sarcasm in her voice. 'I have gone from seeing everything to seeing nothing at all.'

'Well, Tala,' Rollo said, 'that is because you are leading me around all the same places that you have been frequenting with us pixikins.'

'Leading you?' Tala retorted. 'Hah! But, you are supposed to be my guide. Is it not your responsibility to show me what I need to see?'

'I am afraid that it does not work like that, Tala,' Rollo replied, adding, 'not in the real world, in any case. Your life, your responsibility. I am just here to answer any questions that you may have, and to keep you from getting into any trouble.'

'Well I must say, I do indeed wonder what Cornucopious would have to say about that. My life, my responsibility, indeed. You do know that I am only a child, do you not?' Tala asked, but Rollo scarcely rose to the bait.

'Would you rather I held your hand, and told you

what to do?' Rollo asked, and at this, Tala stormed off in a huff, walking as fast as she could through the woods with Rollo rushing along behind her, scarcely able to keep up.

'You see,' said the tortoise, 'Rollo had made his point loud and clear. Tala had longed all her life for autonomy, and now that she had been given it, she wanted to hide behind familiarity. She did not trust herself to find out the truth for herself. Tala knew that Rollo was right, and this is what had angered her most. Sometimes people prefer not to hear the truth.'

Tala walked and she walked and she walked, without thinking, until she came to the edge of the forest, and then she carried on. She had not come this far since the moment that she had slipped on the banana skin and it had changed her life forever. And it was as she crossed this threshold that she realised that, of course, she needed to go to all the places that she used to go to, to see what these other layers of the universe were like there. To see what had been her life, way back when, or the illusion of her life, as it really was.

VIII

Tala stopped short outside what had been her school. She was a little early, for there was not a person in sight. And so she waited, sitting against the railings. A small part of her thought that everything that she had been through was all some big dream, and that the school bell would ring, and that everything would be just as it always had been. But then she glanced to her left and saw Rollo leaning against the wall. She held her hand up to one side and blocked him from her view, but it was no use. Rollo was there as sure as day is day and night is night. She could sense him. She could even hear what he was thinking.

'Okay,' she said, at last. 'Well, seeing as no one else is around, we might as well make friends again.'

'Jolly good,' he said, as he jumped up onto the ledge beside her, and they remained like that, side by side, chit chat chitting away, until a car pulled up out front, and out hopped Mrs Helliwell.

Tala froze to the spot. This would be the real test: whether Mrs Helliwell could see her or not, and, further, whether Tala should, strictly speaking, be slouched out in front of the school railings, in a torn red dress, no less. And just as she was pondering this predicament, a being came into view beside Mrs Helliwell. A magnificent being. A being with wings. Tala gasped. The angel, in turn, gasped. And then it was Rollo's turn to gasp.

Mrs Helliwell appeared to be the only one who was unaffected by this sequence of events.

'I told you,' said the tortoise, with a hint of humour in his voice, 'that the humans are the densest of the lot.'

Indeed, Mrs Helliwell picked out a key from her handbag, unlocked the gates, and in general, carried on about her day-to-day business, completely and utterly oblivious to everything that was going on right beside her.

'Hi,' Tala said.

'Hello indeed,' replied the angel. 'This is a most unusual turn of events.'

'I rather think it is,' Tala concurred. 'Now tell me, can she see me?' Tala asked, as she pointed at Mrs Helliwell.

'It would appear not,' replied the angel.

'And can you see him?' Tala asked, pointing towards Rollo.

'See who?' the angel enquired, and with that, Tala had her answer.

'Hmm,' Tala went on, 'and what about you

CHAPTER VIII

Rollo?'

'Well I can see everything, naturally,' Rollo replied, 'but the trouble is, no one but you can see me.'

'Well, this is a sticky state of affairs,' Tala concluded, and just as the angel was about to reply, he realised that his ward had moved off into the distance.

'Oh, I say,' he said, 'I must be getting on. Do follow, if you may.'

And at this, the angel walked straight through the railings, for the gate that Mrs Helliwell had opened had long since swung shut. Tala opened her mouth wide. She looked at Rollo, and Rollo nodded, and then she proceeded to do exactly the same thing: straight through the railings and out the other side. She turned back to face them, and then grabbed ahold of one of them with her hands. And then she let go of it and swished her arm clean through it. It was all an illusion. The railings could be there or not be there, as she saw fit, she realised. Now, things were getting very interesting. Everything that Tala had ever believed was based on nothing. It was all an illusion. She did the same through a wall, and went straight into one of the classrooms, and then back out again. Of course,

she could have done this back in the realm of the
pixikins, but she hadn't tried. Why would she, after
all? Why would she question what she had always
known to be – or rather assumed to be – true?

IX

'Ah, there you are,' Tala said to the angel, as she walked, through a wall, into Mrs Helliwell's classroom.

It was scarcely a moment after dawn and Mrs Helliwell had come in early to catch up on her marking – or rather – had left it rather late to do all the marking that was required for that very day. *How hypocritical*, Tala mused, as she remembered being told off by Mrs Helliwell for leaving her homework to the last minute, but then she remembered her pledge to herself, and decided not to judge. For all she knew, Mrs Helliwell may have had a terrible ordeal to deal with at home, just as Tala used to have on any given day of the week.

'Do come and take a pew,' replied the angel, as he patted a seat next to him, and naturally Rollo helped himself to a seat as well.

'So you are a real life angel?' Tala asked.

'Naturally,' said the angel. 'And you,' he went on, 'you look very much like a human being to me, but tell me, how can it be that you are here in our dimension?'

And of course, it was a very long story to tell, but Tala told it all, leaving out nothing, and the angel listened attentively, not interrupting even once, not shaking his head in disapproval or disbelief – as would almost certainly have been the case had she been talking to one of her own kind. No. He knew that she was telling the truth, and he waited until she had reached the point where Mrs Helliwell had stepped out of the car, before he launched into his own story.

'There are many types of angels,' he told Tala, 'and I so happen to be a guardian angel. That means that I have been with Mrs Helliwell since the moment that she was born, and I shall remain with her right up until and beyond her death, helping her transition into whatever comes next.'

'Oh my,' Tala replied, 'and has Mrs Helliwell done something particularly special to warrant such attention?'

'Oh no,' the angel replied, 'or yes, rather. What I mean to say is that each and every one of you is special, in your very own unique way, and so each and every one of you deserves your very own guardian angel.'

'You mean, even the baddies?' Tala asked.

'Especially the baddies,' the angel laughed. 'They need us more than most, they are just more cut off from hearing what we have to tell them.

They carry little faith. They may have been through so much bad themselves that they fail to see the good anymore. But we never give up on them.'

'Never?' Tala asked, incredulously.

'Never. Each time they hurt someone else, they hurt themselves much more, you see.'

'Oh,' Tala said, and she reflected on that time that she had pulled her best friend's ponytail.

She had pulled it so hard that she had nearly ripped it out, and everyone had shouted at her that she was a brute, and she had shouted right back that they were even bigger brutes. The real anguish, however, had come that night when she got home, and she could not sleep, and then the sadness had turned into anger – anger at herself, and anger at her friend for making her behave in that brutish way. And why, the very next day, she had been picked on – quite unexpectedly – on her way to school, in a completely, or a seemingly, unrelated occurrence. She could see how a cycle like that could grow and grow, day upon day and night upon night. You hurt someone. You feel remorse or anger, or worse, you feel nothing. Someone else hurts you. You deserved it, but it makes you even more angry. You do not see the link between what you did and what they have done, and so you hurt them right back, even more. It was exhausting just thinking about it. But there must be a way to break this cycle?

'You see,' said the tortoise, 'Tala was beginning to understand the law of cause and effect, or tit for tat, or whatever you like to call it. She was beginning to see that she could spend her life enmeshed in this trap, or that she could choose to break free from it. She could rise above it by simply choosing not to engage. Someone hurts you. You do not need to hurt them back. Tit, but no tat, creates no more tit. Do you follow?'

And it was about then that Tala noticed a cat sitting on Mrs Helliwell's feet.

'Now this is most unorthodox,' she said. 'Pets have never been allowed here before.'

'Oh that,' replied the angel, 'well that is not a cat-cat, if you follow my drift, that is something altogether different.'

'Not a cat-cat?' Tala enquired with widening eyes, but at this Rollo intervened.

'Do not trouble yourself with that right now,' he said. 'I can assure you that we will cover that a little later.'

And with that, Tala took the opportunity to ask some pressing questions. She found out that guardian angels help their wards in specific ways, always watching, always guiding. Some people are more highly attuned to receiving guidance than others. It could come in the form of a sudden flash of inspiration, for example, or a felt sense. Knowing something all of a sudden without knowing why, or a thought from within. That would be an angel whispering into your ear. Some receive guidance whilst never knowing that they are, whilst others can even feel, or sense, or, in rare cases, see their angels – as humans with wings, or as light, for the angels have many forms. They are seen as the seer wishes to see them. And at this Tala stepped back and perceived the very same angel as a great circle of splendiferous light.

And as for the other types of angels: these are the mighty Archangels, and these particular angels are there to help whenever they are called upon. It does not matter how many times you call them, they will always come, and they can help many people at a time.

'Say you were in London and I in Northumberland,' said the angel, 'or that I was in Australia, and you in Timbuktu, why, they could help us both at the same time. Time and space are an illusion after all.'

And with this, Tala said out loud a name that was very dear to her heart, a name that she had always known without knowing why.

'Archangel Gabriel,' she said.

'Who me?' came the unexpected reply, as Archangel Gabriel appeared before her very eyes.

And by and by she found out that Gabriel was there to help her with her purpose in life, and may well have given her a little nudge in the direction of the banana skin, knowing, as always, the greater good that it would bring.

'Well I never,' Tala declared, and then they called in some others: Archangel Michael, why, he could be called upon any time to help shield her from negativity – both her own and from others – and Metatron, for wisdom.

And Tala could have spent an eternity sitting there with what seemed like her oldest and dearest of friends, had that wretched bell not rung. And no sooner had it done so, than great hordes of children – Tala's classmates, no less – came scurrying into the room. Tala was scarcely prepared for such an explosion of the senses, for it was not just her classmates that had entered the room. Oh no. There were angels aplenty, and other grown up humans that she had never seen before, and animals – animals everywhere – of every type. A veritable whirlwind of activity. Whisperings here, and helping hands there. Tala pinched herself to check if she was dreaming, but no, this dream was real. It was her previous existence that had been the dream.

X

Tala had been so busy enjoying herself and marvelling in her new-found knowledge that it did not dawn upon her – at least not until they walked out of the school that afternoon – that she was the only human being who did not appear to have a guardian angel, and naturally this made her rather sad. *There must be something wrong with me*, she reflected, but no sooner had she thought it, than it occurred to her that if angels cannot see the pixikin realm, why, her angel must have lost her about the time that she entered into that realm. She looked at Rollo and Rollo nodded in agreement.

'But where is my guardian angel now?' Tala asked.

'I am afraid that I do not know the answer to that, Tala,' Rollo replied, with a hint of embarrassment in his voice, for the words, 'I do not know,' had seldom featured in his vocabulary before now.

'But I thought that the pixikins knew everything – the all-knowing, the omnipotent...' Tala replied, but Rollo cut her short.

'Be that as it may, Tala, you must remember that this has never happened before, and besides, even when we think we know it all, we must always be prepared for the unexpected. What say we find out together?'

'If only I had a name, I could call her,' Tala went on, and then it dawned upon her, that she was not in this alone.

'Archangel Gabriel,' she said out loud, 'please help me find my guardian angel,' and no sooner had she said it, than a shimmering light appeared. The light spoke:

'Think of where your angel would have last seen you, Tala; your angel will have been looking for you ever since.'

And that was all that Tala needed to hear. Of course it was so.

'Thank you Gabriel,' she said, and the light evaporated as quickly as it had appeared, and Tala quickened her pace.

'We must get back to the forest,' she said, as she walked straight into and through a brick wall.

'Quite the little expert,' Rollo joked, as he followed her through into someone's living room.

'Well, we'll get there so much quicker if we cut right through,' Tala replied.

Only the further they went – into and out of people's houses – Tala began to feel rather like an intruder, and it was then that she realised that she should not use these new-found powers for her own gain in this way. She should use them only when they were called for to serve others, or when necessary to get to something. *But public properties – say parks and railings – that is still fine*, Tala reflected, for she was laying down her boundaries of what was right and wrong – for her.

They reached the forest at dusk, and Tala made her way straight to the banana skin. It was still there. A little blackened maybe, but there nonetheless.

'How strange it must have been, to watch something all your life, and for it to up and vanish into thin air,' Tala said sadly, adding, 'I do hope that my angel is not sad.'

They then proceeded to trudge around the forest, silently, side-by-side.

'If we want to go to the next dimension today, Tala, we shall have to leave before the light is gone,' Rollo said, but Tala would not hear of it.

'My angel would not give up on me, so I will not give up on my angel,' she said.

And so on they went, but not a soul was in sight, and several hours passed in this way. It was as Tala could barely stand for being so tired that, at last, she decided that she needed to have a little sleep. They had come full circle, after all, and were back where they had started, at the banana skin.

Tala lay down beside it. She went straight into a dreamlike state. She was not aware of whether she was asleep or awake, but she suddenly felt a presence beside her. She opened her eyes and the most beautiful woman that she had ever seen was seated beside her on the ground.

'Tala, my dear,' she said, and just as Tala was about to ask who this wonderful woman was, she realised that she was surrounded by light, and had the most magnificent wings.

Tala's eyes filled with tears of joy.

'Are you who I think you are?' she asked, and at this, the angel's eyes too were filled with tears.

'You can see me?' the angel asked, and at this, Tala flung her arms around her, and they stayed like this, as Tala kept weeping a river of tears.

But these were not tears of sadness. No. These were tears of joy, for Tala had never felt so happy in all her life. All those times that she had cried for being alone and unwanted, and here she was, surrounded by love. Whatever happened in the future, knowing this would make a difference to her life. Tala would never again feel alone or cut off from the world.

XI

Tala and her guardian angel – Geranium, after the flower – stayed up all night talking, reminiscing, for naturally, Geranium had lived through it all: the good times, the bad times, the decidedly average times, side-by-side with Tala. And as morning came they went for a walk. Geranium showed Tala all the ways that she had learnt to communicate with her, and Tala got a sense of how the messages had come through. Little nudges here and there. Little sensations. Flashes of wisdom, which she chose to act upon or ignore, dependent on her mood. Knowing this, too, would make a difference. Tala would never again turn a blind eye to this guidance, even if it was not entirely what she wanted to hear. Even if it forced her to go out and do things in the big wide world when all she really wanted to do was to sit at home in her nightie drinking hot cups of milk.

And when they found their way back to the banana skin, Rollo was sitting on top of it with his hand held up to his face, tapping his index finger to his lip, in mock boredom. Tala smiled at the sight of him, and then her smile dropped a little.

'It is time to move on, isn't it?' she said.

Of course, Geranium could not see Rollo, but understood quite well what was going on.

'Do not be sad Tala,' she said, 'for I shall be right beside you.'

'But not like this,' Tala said, as she held on to Geranium's hand.

'Well, maybe not, but just think, we will always have this moment, and besides, you will be more attuned to me now.'

'But...' Tala said, for there were a million and one questions swirling around in her head, but the truth of it was, not one of them – be it Geranium, Rollo, or Tala – really knew what was going to happen in the next realm, let alone when Tala got back to her own dimension. Would she be the same as when she had left? Would this all just be some elaborate dream? But now that they had started their descent, they could scarcely stop. It was time to move on, and Tala was old enough and wise enough to know that. She hugged Geranium, and then she picked out the bubble tube from her pocket.

On the count of three, Rollo and Tala blew and they blew and they blew; they jumped inside their respective bubbles, swirled around, and hey presto, they were back out in the Milky Way. They did a couple of laps around the stars, the moon, and the sun, and then they swirled around again, and, boom, they were back.

'Geranium,' Tala said, as her eyes filled with tears, for although she could not see her, she could sense that she was there.

'Come now, you must rest,' Rollo told Tala, and she leant right back, and fell into a deep sleep.

And when she opened her eyes, she knew that she had changed a little. Something had permanently implanted itself inside of her. She could not say what. Experience, wisdom, understanding, whatever it was, Tala had grown, inside.

'And now?' she said, turning to Rollo, but Rollo merely reflected it back at her.

'Yes, now what, Tala? What shall we do?' he said, and Tala rolled her eyes a little, and began to walk.

They walked all the way through the forest, then through the streets, and back to school, and, although there was a veritable flurry of activity, nothing could see her. She had not found what she was looking for – not in this dimension, anyway.

'Well, there is clearly nothing to see,' she said. 'Not here at least. I need to be somewhere altogether different. Angels, any clue?'

And then her mind was filled with a thought. It was crystal clear. *I can go wherever I want. I am not constrained by the laws of physics.*

'Take me to the mountains,' she said, on a whim – to whom she was not sure, her Self maybe – and then she was in the Himalayas.

She put each hand up to the opposite arm, rubbing them, before it dawned on her that, in actual fact, she was not cold. She had seen the snowy peaks and her mind had told her that she should be cold, but she was altogether fine. In fact, she wanted for nothing at all. Everything was exactly as it should be. She sat down, cross-legged on the ground, marvelling at the view around her, and then she moved into a state of absolute peace. Everything around her was a part of her, or rather, she was a part of it all. The mountains. The sky. The birds. The trees. There was nothing to distinguish between any of it. It was all the same thing. Breathing the same breath.

It could have been hours, days, or weeks before she moved, but slowly she became aware of someone sitting next to her. She was back in her body.

'I rather like it here too,' came the voice, a gentle

voice.

It was a young man with long, flowing black hair, sitting cross-legged beside her, dressed in nothing but a small sheet around his waist – despite the cold, which she could no longer feel, in any case.

'Where did you come from?' Tala asked.

'Who me?' he replied, as he shouted out loud from the opposite peak.

But he was still beside her too.

'Oh, I can be in many places at the same time,' he continued, 'sitting here, marvelling at life, or helping out humans – truth seekers – who want and need my guidance and blessing.'

Tala was speechless and in awe.

'See,' he said, as he cut into a living room, taking Tala with him. A man was sitting there, deep in contemplation, and calling out for help and guidance. Tala's new friend placed his hand on his head, wishing him well. Of course, this man could not see them, but something inside of him changed, as if he could feel the healing energy he had received.

And then they were back on the mountain, or rather, they had never really left the mountain.

'But how can it be that you can do all these things?' she asked. 'For at first glance, you could be a real man.'

'Well, once upon a time, I was,' he explained, 'but gradually, and through many lifetimes, I kept working hard to understand the incomprehensible, and one day, well, I just remained as I am now. Never ageing. My personal work was done. I ascended. And there are many just like me who too have come to this state of realisation. And now, well, now it is time for us to help out others on their path. That is why I stay here.'

Tala thought about this long and hard.

'But do people know you are helping?' she asked.

'Many, no,' he said. 'But all the more reason to

keep helping. To shed a little light here and there. But things are changing, Tala, there are some people who are starting to understand, and this is how the work can spread, how people can be freed from their misery.'

Tala took a little while to take this all in. Other lives. Being in several places at the same time. Never ageing. Helping to free people. And then it hit her, her life, until now, had been some sort of prison. She had felt stuck, and unable to move. But really that was only a small part of the whole. Seeing the wider picture would reduce the strain of the smaller picture. How could it not?

'You are a part of this journey now, Tala. There is so much that you can do, you must just believe in yourself even if others don't, or if it seems like they don't.'

Tala fell silent. It was rather a tall order, but how could she know all of this and not do anything with it? Enough had been said.

'You see,' said the tortoise, 'Tala was beginning to get a grasp of what path she must take. She could not be told it all in one fell swoop. It would have been too much for her, scaring her off the path. No. She was learning in increments, as it should be. For a dense human at least,' he added, with a chuckle.

Tala re-entered into that magical state, as she sat side-by-side with the ascended master, and when she came to, she saw Rollo sitting in front of her. Her new friend had gone, but she felt certain that she would be calling upon him again, one of these days.

XII

You know the drill by now. Tala and Rollo planted themselves back in the forest, for wherever they were going next, Tala had the foresight to know that starting in the snowy peaks of the Himalayas might put her at a disadvantage. They re-bubbled up, did a swift tour of the Milky Way, and, boom, they were down on the next rung of the ladder. A short sleep later, and Tala instinctively walked towards the edge of the forest.

'A horse parade,' she said with glee, as they reached the roadside, and a cavalry so happened to be going past.

'They used to let us stand outside school and watch this,' Tala went on, adding, 'They must be going in that direction now.'

Only, as she spoke, she became aware of something slightly different. She could not quite place it at first. There were more horses than humans. That was it, and they were all crammed together like she had never seen before. And then she thought that she saw a horse looking at her. Yes, it caught her eye, and their eyes locked. The horse appeared to look as stunned as she was.

'Wait!' she called out, as she ran after them, and

several of the horses turned around to face her, whilst the others, the ones with the humans sitting on top of them, kept on going, regardless.

Tala's mind was spinning. *What is this?* And then she remembered Rollo's words: 'That is not a cat-cat,' he had said, had he not?

She turned to look at him.

'These are not horse-horses, are they?' she said, and he nodded in the affirmative.

'So what, indeed, pray tell, are they then?' she asked, but very much to her surprise, one of the horses replied.

'Excuse me, Ma'am, to whom are you speaking?' she said.

'Oh,' Tala replied. 'Well, I have come to expect the unexpected, but I was not expecting that.'

'I might say the very same thing,' the horse replied, 'but please, we are straying from our path. Since you seem to be in our dimension, please do jump on board.'

'But...' Tala said, 'I have never ridden a horse. I wanted to, but I was just never allowed.'

'Well now is your chance,' the horse helpfully suggested.

'But do I not need a saddle?' Tala went on. 'Or perhaps a riding hat or a...?' But then she broke off mid-sentence.

After all that she had been through, you would hardly think that she would be afraid of a horse. She picked Rollo up, and put him in her pocket, then placed a hand on the back of the horse, leapt up and swung a leg over. Of all the things that she thought she would be doing that day, bare horseback riding was not one of them, but she took to it rather like a natural.

'Giddy up,' Tala said, as she pressed her feet into the horse's sides, but the horse just came to a standstill.

'You have been watching too many movies, young lady,' she said. 'I am in charge here.'

And that put Tala in her place. But she was a pleasant horse nonetheless, and as they trotted along, amidst the procession, they took the opportunity to find out a little more about one another. The horse explained – right from the horse's mouth, if you will excuse the pun – that she was a spirit animal, rather than an animal-animal, if you will. This meant that although she shared attributes with the real horse, she was operating in another dimension, and she was assigned to a particular human – much like a guardian angel is, Tala reflected. But as well as sharing attributes with the animal kingdom, she also shares attributes with the human to which she is assigned. So, in this case, her ward had a joie de vivre: an indestructible passion that drove her forward in life.

'But all these people riding horses,' Tala said, 'seem to have a horse as a spirit animal.'

'Well, yes,' the horse conceded, 'and the reason for that is that the horse-like characteristics of these particular humans – strong, driven, on a quest to be free – make them naturally inclined to like horses, hence they chose this as a profession. Do you follow?'

'I think so,' Tala replied.

'Thus a fiery, powerful, self-confident being,' the horse went on, 'might be inclined to have a lion for a spirit animal, and a rather nice, but slow-to-do individual, a sloth, and so on and so forth.'

And at this Tala laughed.

'But let us not be fooled,' the horse added, 'for a sloth too has its attributes: self-acceptance, for one. Now how many of you humans can say that?'

'So Mrs Helliwell had a cat. That is because she is clever, and able to stand on her own two feet, as all good teachers should be,' Tala said.

'Well, I cannot say that I know who Mrs Helliwell

is,' the horse replied, 'but that sounds about right to me.'

And by and by they made it to the school. As suspected, her classmates were all standing at the roadside, waiting to catch a glimpse of the passing procession, but of course, it was not just her classmates this time. It was lions and tigers and giraffes. You name it.

Tala thanked her new equestrian friend for the ride, and hopped off. She came face-to-face with a bear and made to run, in spite of herself, but it was too late.

'Hey you!' he called out. 'Stop running away from your fears.'

'Ah, oh, okay,' Tala replied, nonplussed.

'I ain't gonna hurt ya, if that's what ya thinking,' the bear went on.

'Well, you know, I have seen some wildlife programmes, and you can never be too sure,' Tala replied.

'Those'll be my ancestors – the bear-bears,' the bear replied. 'They need to survive out back, just as you do, but me, I'm pure spirit. I ain't lookin for no ruckus. Here, come on board.'

And with that, Tala cautiously jumped on his back – piggyback style.

'You see,' the bear went on, 'I don't take no stick from nobody,' as other spirit animals moved out of his way. 'If someone is mistreating me, or anyone else for that matter, well, you'll pretty soon find that I step in.'

And with that the bear roared and the whole animal kingdom turned to look at him.

'See,' he went on.

And just then they were interrupted by a ruckus in the playground, and the bear ran straight over to Tala's friend, Timmy.

'It looks like we're needed,' he said, and although Timmy could not hear him, just having the bear beside him was enough to spur him on, and he did what was necessary to break up the fight.

'And that,' said the bear, 'is how we roll.'

Tala spent the rest of the day bonding with the various members of the animal kingdom, learning more about them, and indeed the qualities of her classmates too, but it had not escaped her attention, this time, that she was without her spirit animal. A kindly tiger escorted her back to the forest, and once she was there, she sat beside the banana skin, patiently waiting. She knew that she would be reunited in time. Rollo sat beside her, and by and by, they both lay back and drifted off to sleep.

It was an otherworldly humming sound that woke her up. She thought that perhaps she was dreaming, and so she lay there listening with her eyes closed, and then the humming sound turned into squeaks.

'Rollo, can you hear that?' she whispered, but Rollo was out cold, or at least pretending to be. He did not want to ruin Tala's special moment.

She sat upright, and over the treetops she saw a wave-like motion, coming towards her. Up and down, it went. Leaping out above the treetops, and then back down below. Up and down. It was not until it got a little closer that Tala realised that it was a dolphin. She clapped her hands together with excitement, and the dolphin let out a little chattering sound, as he swooped right down towards her. He halted directly in front of her, without saying a word – for words were not needed at a magical moment like this – and then he turned his back to her. The message was clear. Tala grabbed ahold of his fin, and then up and off they went into the sky. They were swimming

through the air – above the treetops – by the light
of the moon. And they swam and they swam and
they swam, out of the forest, past Tala's old house,
past all the places that she used to frequent.

Tala saw it all, with a bird's-eye view, and
from that perspective, she saw her life, both as
she thought it had been, and as it really was.
She realised that, yes, she had been through
difficulties, but she also saw that she could let
them consume her, or rise above them, as she was
now. See the wider picture. She thought about the
qualities of the dolphin as they went about their
business – inner strength, for example – well, she
had that one already, playfulness too. But what

about protection, of both herself and others, and cooperation with kindred spirits? She saw how she could cultivate these further in her own life. Yes, this dolphin would teach her to draw upon the qualities that she needed most, when she needed them, and most of all to put her trust in herself.

And they swam right through until dawn, without uttering a single word, just enjoying each moment for what it was. The dolphin dropped her back at the banana skin, and swam around her, playfully, as Tala and Rollo prepared for the next stage in their mission. This time, Tala was not sad to say goodbye, for she was beginning to understand that everything that she had been through, every encounter that she had had, would live on inside of her through all of time. And besides, she did not need to see the dolphin with her eyes to know that he would be there, click-clack-clicking away beside her, whenever she needed him – for the layers of the universe are not so very far apart as she had once thought.

XIII

'Hello, hello,' Tala called out loud, as she came to from her post-travel slumber. 'Is there anybody out there?' For instinctively, she felt that she could spend an age working out who or what she was supposed to meet in this next realm, or, she could sit back and let them come to her.

'Tired are we?' Rollo asked, with a smirk on his face.

'Well seeing as you are clearly not going to help me...' Tala retorted, but she was stopped short mid-sentence, because already, her ploy had worked.

She heard a series of voices, rather high-pitched, shrill voices; they were getting closer.

'It came from over there,' said voice number one.

'Oh no it didn't, it was there,' said voice number two.

'No, no, no. You both have it wrong. It is this way, come on,' came the third, and just then, a trio of fairies came into view.

One of them was rather like a butterfly, only with the body of a human; the others were more like mini humans with the wings of a dragonfly. Tala sat there watching them. Of course, they saw her, but they were used to seeing humans in the human realm, knowing full well that they could not be seen, and so they carried on about their business, scarcely paying any attention to her.

'Now you've gone and done it,' said fairy two. 'I told you it was that way.'

'But it was this way,' fairy three proclaimed, tightening her fists with exasperation.

'Well, whichever way it was,' fairy one chimed in, 'it does not matter now; whoever called out has long since gone. You should have listened to me.'

'Uh-hum,' Tala cleared her throat, but the fairies carried on bickering.

She did it again, a little louder.

'Uh-hum.'

And again.

'Uh-hum, hello, it was me-ee.'

And at this, fairy two turned to face her.

'Excuse me,' she said, 'we are trying to have a conversation here, if you don't mind,' but no sooner had she said it, than it dawned on her who she was talking to.

'Ahhh!' she screamed, flailing her little arms in the air.

Fairy three stepped in. She flew right up to Tala.

'Excuse me,' she said, with her hands on her hips, 'are you talking to us?'

'Well, yes, as a matter of fact I am,' Tala replied. 'I am ever so pleased to make your acquaintance at last.'

'And pray do tell, how can it be that you – a mere human – can see us?' fairy one asked.

'Well, it is a long story,' Tala replied, bracing herself. 'But suffice to say, that I am in your dimension now.'

'Huh,' fairy two laughed. 'Did you hear that? This little girl thinks she is one of us.'

And at that fairy three flew over and landed clean on Tala's shoulder.

Now they knew that something serious was going on, for occasionally humans do get to see glimpses of fairies, but this – liaising with, and being able to physically touch one – was most definitely a first.

'Well I never,' the fairies said in unison.

And that is when they sat down in front of Tala and proceeded to hear it all. It was not without interruption, though.

'Uh, hello, you slipped on a banana skin, isn't that a bit of a cliché?' asked fairy two.

'More like an excuse to be a litter bug, look at that rotting skin over there, it's a disgrace,' fairy one chimed in.

'For the fairies,' said the tortoise, 'are very protective of nature. It is where they draw their breath from. So, if you want to be friends with the fairies, then you must never drop your rubbish outside of a rubbish bin, do you hear?'

When Tala got to the part about meeting the pixikins, she was met with even more incredulity.

'A pixikin?' said fairy two. 'I never heard of a pixikin.'

'Well, there is one beside you right now,' Tala clarified.

'And pigs might fly,' fairy two retorted.

'Rollo, is there anything that you can do to prove it?' Tala asked, as she began to wonder if she would ever get through her tale, but it was no use, Rollo just shrugged his shoulders.

'This is part of your mission, Tala,' he said, 'to spread the word the best way that you know how.'

And then it dawned upon Tala that this was the first time that she had met with resistance and judgement since her journey began, and she realised that she must be getting close to the human realm, for both of these traits were things that she had only ever seen in her own kind. She took a different tack. She realised that she could not just tell people these extraordinary things and expect them to believe them, with no experience of it themselves. Instead, she focused on what they could understand, and, more, took an interest in them.

'Well, here I am now,' she said. 'How I came to be here is a bit of a mystery, but I am on a journey to learn what I can, and,' she added, 'I believe that I have much to learn from you that I could take back to my own kind.'

The fairies moved to the side and had a little conference. They kept looking Tala up and down, and then turning back to face one other.

'We have decided,' said fairy three, upon re-entering the fore, 'that you are a good little girl.'

'Well,' fairy two added, 'good enough, could do a bit better.'

'We can see,' said fairy one, 'that you are kind to animals, and do not harm the environment.'

'Apart from that banana skin there,' fairy two added. 'And look see, there is a shadow there,' she said to the others, as she pointed into thin air beside Tala's head. 'She must have dropped some litter once or twice in her life.'

How they could know all of this, just by looking at her, was beyond Tala.

'But by and large,' fairy three went on, 'your colours are good.'

'My colours?' Tala asked, nonplussed.

'Yes, and for this reason, we have decided to help you,' fairy three concluded, adding, 'Now lie down, over there, please.'

Tala looked at Rollo, and Rollo gave an encouraging nod, and then she went and settled herself, flat on her back on a bed of leaves, in between a circle of trees. She closed her eyes, and a strange but pleasant feeling came over her. It was as if she were connected to the earth by roots. She lay there, motionless, and felt the air around her move. It was the fairies at work.

'Here's a bad bit,' fairy two said, and Tala felt a moment of tension, before it rippled away and off into the far distance, never to be seen again.

'Ooh, and another,' fairy two went on, and Tala felt the same sensation again.

They were working their way around her body, but they were not physically touching her. No. It was as if they were changing the very air, the energy around her, and the deeper they went, the lighter Tala felt. Little memories surfaced here and there of some of the things that Tala was more ashamed off, but off they went into the distance. There was no point holding on to that pain anymore.

'All done,' fairy three announced, and with that

Tala felt able to move again. She sat up, and as she did, she felt lighter, less constricted. She had let go of so much in such a short space of time.

'Now what was that?' Tala asked, and by and by she learnt that the fairies could see the energy around her as colours, letting them know exactly what was going on inside of her: what type of thoughts she had, what sort of mood she was in, how healthy she was, how clever she was.

And not only that, they – the fairies – had the ability to help people clear the negativity within them, by doing exactly what they had just done to Tala. Say when people are out in nature walking around, the fairies might hover just beside them and have a little clean – if and only if they deem that person to be worthy.

Of course, it was all rather a lot for Tala to take in. She understood, and had, indeed, experienced the positive effects herself, but it is hard to fathom something completely unless you have experienced it for yourself, and as if sensing this, fairy number three suggested a little outing.

'It is time for you, young lady, to go back to school,' she said.

XIV

Tala, together with the three fairies, and – unbeknownst to the fairies – Rollo, positioned themselves at the back of the classroom. They chose a particularly boring class – Pythagoras' theorem in mathematics – on purpose, so that they would not be tempted to listen at all. No. They were there to create their own lesson. But, for the lesson to be effective they needed white walls and people.

'Now look at the top of that girl's head,' fairy three instructed, as she pointed to a girl sitting near the wall, 'and tell me what you see.'

Tala paused for a long while before answering.

'Hair,' she said at last, unable to come up with any other answer, to which, the fairies all let out a little explosion of laughter.

'Hair?' fairy two shrieked. 'Now state the obvious why don't you.'

'But that is what I see,' Tala responded, her feelings a little hurt.

'Perhaps you could try a little harder,' fairy one unhelpfully suggested.

'Ooh,' Tala said, 'there is a crumb in her hair.'

And of course, this time the fairies laughed even louder and harder still.

'Focus,' fairy three said at last, 'or rather don't focus. Look, but don't look.'

Tala looked at Rollo and Rollo just cheerily smiled back, and then she turned back to what she was doing. She looked at the girl's head. Yes, there was hair; yes, there was a crumb, and then a fly landed on her head, but by now, she knew better than to comment on that. She just sat there. *When in doubt, do nowt*, kept whirring around in her head. She softened her gaze a little, and found that she was looking without really looking; it was as if she were seeing out of her peripheral vision, rather than head on. And just then a ring of light appeared around the girl's head. It was visible against the white wall. Tala gasped and looked directly at it, only it was gone. She did the same again, once, twice, thrice, and by now she understood. *Never look directly at it*. She held the gaze, and then she saw colour emerging too.

She turned to face the fairies.

'Now let me guess,' said fairy two sarcastically, 'you have spotted a head louse?'

And at this the fairies laughed again, but Tala did not rise to the bait.

'Orange,' she said.

And that stopped them in their tracks, for Tala

was a quick learner.

'Yes Tala,' fairy three encouraged, 'and from that you can deduce that this is a kind-hearted, sociable little girl.'

'What about her?' fairy one asked, pointing at another girl.

'Blue,' Tala responded, after a long pause.

'Ah, a good communicator, perhaps a little poet in the making,' fairy three explained.

And round they went until Tala had seen all the colours of the rainbow, and was really starting to grasp how this new-found knowledge could help her to understand people better. Another tool in her toolbox, so to speak. And she learnt that auras are not static either, they can change with the thoughts and experiences of the person, and that they can also be felt. Tala covered her eyes as she walked towards different people in the classroom, and just by standing near them, she was able to get a sense of the type of person they might be, or the type of mood that they were in.

Back in the forest, Tala looked at the trees, and saw energy all around them, and realised that every living thing has an energy field. Every living thing has its place on this earth. They got back to the spot where they started, and Tala

explained that it was time for her to leave; this time there was no bickering, or joking around, for the fairies had become rather fond of Tala, just as Tala had become rather fond of her new friends. They landed on the palm of her hand and danced around in a little circle, singing a blessing for Tala on her travels. Tala, for her part, promised to never throw a piece of rubbish again, and to always look after the environment, and then she upped and inned to her bubble, as the fairies watched with jaws ajar, and – poof – she was gone, back out into the Milky Way.

XV

Tala already knew that they were close to the human realm, and so when she made her way back into town with Rollo, she was not surprised at all to see what, at first sight, she thought were ordinary human beings locking eyes with her. She locked eyes right back. Only little by little, she noticed that for every so-called human being that she locked eyes with, there was one that completely passed her by. Curious. She did not wish to make a spectacle of herself, and so bided her time carefully, observing. This one sees me; this one doesn't. This one sees me; this one doesn't. She needed time out to think – for Rollo was clearly not going to give her any answers, she knew that by now.

'Afraid not,' Rollo replied, having read her thoughts. 'There are some things that are just better found out alone.'

'What, you mean, like everything,' Tala retorted, 'and please stop doing that.'

And by that, of course, she meant reading her thoughts, but she knew, as she said it, that that would be a physical impossibility, for it came as naturally to Rollo as hearing the words that she said.

They continued their journey in silence. Tala was heading straight for a little playground near her childhood home, a place she used to go, to get away from it all when things became too much. *It would be nice and quiet there now*, she reflected, for the sun had scarcely risen. She walked straight in through the unopened gate, and was surprised to see an old man sitting with his back to her on the very swing that she had spent hours wiling away the time on.

'Oh bother,' she said out loud, and, very much to her surprise, the old man turned around to face her.

She froze to the spot, stunned. Everything

felt somehow unreal. She looked at the man and had a strong sense of déjà vu. She had seen him before and yet not seen him. She knew him and yet did not know him. She racked her brains, and suddenly it all fell into place. There was a photo in her house of an old man tickling her feet as a baby, and this was the very man sitting in front of her. She was sure of it. She knew the photo well, for it had often made her smile. The look of affection in his eyes. Only, the reason she did not know him, was that he was long since deceased.

A thousand thoughts ran through her mind. *I am not dead am I?* she wondered first of all, and then, *or have I simply lost the plot? Perhaps I am making this whole thing up.* But, just as she was looking at him, he was looking at her.

'Can you see me, Tala?' he asked at last, breaking the silence.

'I can,' she said, 'and I know you from a photograph. My parents told me that you are my Great Uncle Ashley, but it cannot really be you, can it, for you have not aged a bit?'

'Oh, I have crossed over to the other side, Tala. Soon after you were born, in fact, but I decided to hang around a bit. I knew what you were born into, and I knew that you would need my support.'

'Hang around?' Tala asked.

And at this, her Great Uncle Ashley introduced her to all that there was to know about the realm of the Spirit Guides: spirit entities assigned to you before or after birth to guide you in specific areas. Some have only existed in spirit form whereas others have had previous lifetimes on earth such as deceased ancestors who have chosen to stay behind to guide and support you. They undertake training themselves so that they may best be of help to you and guide you in much the same way as your guardian angel might: through sudden insights, gut feelings and dreams.

'And pray, where do you take your training?' Tala asked.

'Well, let's just say, it is a little like school, or should I say sky school,' Great Uncle Ashley replied, adding, 'Time is not so important up there, and passes much quicker than you humans think. I could be having a lesson, and feel your call of help and be with you in scarcely a nanosecond.'

'Oh my,' Tala said, 'but you mean to tell me that you do all this just for me?'

'Yes, Tala, I will be with you throughout your life.'

'But why?' Tala asked, nonplussed.

'Because I care about you, and besides, you and I are not so very dissimilar, if the truth be known. Perhaps that is why I felt an affinity with you from the very first time that I saw you.'

'And why I smile every time I see your photograph,' Tala added.

'I knew the type of work that you would do,' Great Uncle Ashley went on, 'work that I started and could not complete in my lifetime, and that I could somehow help you, help guide you when times were tough to stay on the path.'

'But what is my path?' Tala asked, and at this Great Uncle Ashley merely let out a big smile, and said:

'You will find out soon enough.'

'For no one can tell you your destiny outright,' said the tortoise. 'That has to come from within. Let's just say that it is stored in a little storehouse up in the sky, but the key is only given to those who have done the work. And how many of you humans really do the work?'

And from here, they moved on to all that Tala had been through since her departure from the world as she knew it, on that slippery, old banana skin. Great Uncle Ashley had seen her vanish into clean air, and had been visiting all her favourite haunts since, in the hope of finding out what had become of her. And now, here she was. He could she that she had grown a thousandfold, even if she did not yet know it. He could see that the time was ripe for her to step into her power, that she would no longer be held back by the petty complaints of those who did not understand her. Tala was on the edge of a new dawn. The world was on the edge of a new dawn, and whether she liked it or not, Tala would have her part to play.

XVI

Tala's journey through the realms was drawing to a close. As she bade her great uncle farewell, she knew it. And as she spun out into the Milky Way and round and round the stars, the sun, and the moon, she reflected on all that she had been through. Of course, she had absolutely no idea what would happen next, but she was ready to face whatever it was. She felt a mixture of excitement and fear. What would it be like to mix with her own kind again? Would she maintain the experiences that she had been through, or would it soon enough all seem like a distant dream? They took a little longer than usual, really working their way round, working through everything, processing, and when and only when Tala's mind went silent, Rollo did a little thumbs up signal. It was time to re-enter the human realm. Tala took a deep breath and then counted to three, and, boom, she was back.

She opened her eyes, and Rollo was no longer with her, or, at least, she could not see him. She felt a moment of panic, for as much as she had complained about him, she had become rather used to having Rollo by her side. *What would*

Rollo do now? she thought, and immediately it was clear to her that she needed to look after herself, that she needed to rest, for she had taken a small piece of him into her very being, and it had become a part of who she was. A positive voice of authority, if you will.

When she came to, she turned to her side and saw the banana skin. Slowly, she made her way over to it, and picked it up; she pressed it to her heart.

'It did happen,' she said out loud, and in spite of herself, a tear slipped out of her eye.

'And Rollo, you brute,' she added, 'I never got

a chance to thank you. You are not really so bad, after all.'

And as she sat there in stillness, her silent reverie was broken.

'I am so glad that you have finally seen the light,' she heard, in her mind's eye.

It was in her voice, but yet, as if it came from someone else. She looked around and there was no one there, but from the mischievous tone, she knew that it was Rollo. Why, she could still hear his thoughts.

'Rollo, you beast!' she exclaimed.

'Takes one to know one,' she heard back.

'But, where are you?' she asked.

'Over here, by the tree,' came the response, and Tala scanned her eyes around the myriad of trees that were in front of her.

'Can you be a little more precise please?' she asked.

'About 220 degrees due north,' he replied, and Tala instinctively turned to the right position; it was as if she had a built-in compass in her head.

'For Tala's mind by now was tapping into areas that it did not used to access,' explained the tortoise. 'Whereas most of you humans use about ten per cent of your brain, Tala was learning how to use it all: all of those dark nooks and crannies and vessels and pathways. Most of you just accept that they are there doing nothing, but the brave few take steps to ignite what is rightfully yours.'

At first, Tala could not see anything at all, but then she softened her gaze a little, and against the backdrop of the blue sky, a flash of something came into view. It was a ball of fluffy yellow hair. There was no mistaking it.

'Rollo!' she exclaimed, with delight in her voice.

And then she saw another pixikin, and another. Why, there was a huddle of them. For her eyes were slowly acclimatising. She heard a round of applause.

'Cornucopious?' she asked expectantly, 'are you there?' And then a pinpointed wizard hat came into view.

She jumped up and down. Cornucopious jumped up and down. And the more time she spent there, the better her vision adjusted. She saw more of him by the second.

'Tala, you have done it,' Cornucopious said. 'I always knew that you would.'

'I can hear you,' she said, adding, 'I can see you too. Oh Cornucopious, it has been such a journey.'

'I know,' he replied, 'for I have been with you all

the way.'

She went to pick him up, but her hand went straight through him.

'Oh do not let a mere trifle like that get you down,' Cornucopious advised, sensing Tala's slight drop in energy, 'for you have exceeded all of our expectations. Do you not see what a miracle this is? You are a human, back in the human realm, and you have access to all of the realms beyond. You can see us, you can hear us, and you can sense us.'

But Tala was scarcely listening. She was looking intently at Cornucopious, and very slowly she moved her hand towards him again, and, this time, she was able to ruffle the top of his hat.

'You see,' said the tortoise, 'Tala was starting to believe in herself, to believe that anything and everything is possible, that all it takes is a little belief.'

He cleared his throat, before continuing, 'And you could say that it is about time too.'

Before long, Tala turned her attention to each of the realms, one by one. Testing the water, so to speak.

'Geranium?' Tala called out softly, and before

she had even finished speaking, Geranium
appeared before her very eyes.

'Tala, my sweet child,' Geranium softly spoke,
and Tala felt the flutter of her wings against her
skin.

Tala made a dolphin sound, and the call was
reciprocated. She called upon the mystical master
of contemplation and saw a glimpse of him in the
woods, and felt his blessing. She called upon the
fairies and they came flying into view, bowing and
curtsying in mid-air as they reached her. She called
upon her dear Great Uncle Ashley, and he too was
there within just two shakes of a lamb's tail. They
were all there, with her and for her, whenever she
wanted. She was not alone in this world. She was
connected to it all.

Together, as if in procession, they made their
way to the edge of the forest, and then through
the streets. Tala would have to be careful now, an
eight year old girl, seemingly out on the streets on
her own, like this. She would also have to mind
when and how she spoke to her support team. For
in the world, as most people know it, there is scant
regard for people like Tala. Ordinary people do
not understand the incomprehensible, and so they
fight it, try to quash it, say it isn't real, lock people

away because of it, suppress it in any way that they can, when the reality is that it is the only thing that is real.

They went to the busiest place that they could think of, a place where Tala could be anonymous and yet at the same time have the opportunity to view her own kind. A zoo. And as Tala approached it – she saw – not great lines of people queuing up outside, as she was expecting, but great shards of light and swirling spirals of energy. It was as if she could see through an encrypted code all of a sudden. She could see things as they really were. Everyone and everything was made of the same stuff – the same energy – twisted and contorted in different ways, and it was all interacting with each other.

Tala wandered around the zoo in awe. Animals, trees, plants, human beings, it did not matter, there was light around everything. Energy being given, and energy being taken. Tala could flicker her eyes at will and look into and out of the illusive world. She could see both the truth and the illusion. She could see just by looking at a person how far along they had come on their path, the types of thoughts that they had, the aspirations they had, who would help her, who would harm her, who would believe her, and who was ready to be helped. Why, she could even hear their thoughts. She could see their angels, their guides. She could see who was more connected and who was completely shut off from the truth. She could see all of this, just by standing there.

The world was so much richer than she could ever have fathomed. Everyone had their place, no matter what anyone else tried to tell them. Tala sat down on a bench and observed. She had come as far as she needed to come for the next stage in her journey. She had all the tools that she would need to see her through. She had peeled away all the layers of the onion, the negative thoughts of others that had put her down, made her doubt herself. She had stripped herself right down to the core. She had taken something from each of the realms, and it had become a part of who she was. Tala felt a powerful surge of energy in her body, and she was strong enough to hold it.

'You see,' said the tortoise, 'Tala was ready to live the life that she was born to live.'

XVII

'Tala, oh Tala.'

Tala looked up into the sky. She did not know where the voice was coming from. She was back in the depths of the forest by now, for she felt more at home there than she had ever felt at her so-called real home.

'Tala, oh Tala,' it came again, and Tala knelt down on the ground.

'It is time,' the voice said, and Tala held her arms up to the sky.

The tortoise descended from the sky on an enormous beam of effervescent light.

'And for those of you who are not particularly bright,' said the tortoise, 'that tortoise was, of course, me.'

The tortoise stopped short in front of Tala, and as Tala looked directly into his eyes, she felt that he carried within him the knowledge of the whole world, that there was nothing that this wise tortoise did not know. He had seen it all, lived it all. He had been in existence since the beginning of time, and beyond. He had all the answers. He was the sun, the earth, and the moon. He was everything that had ever been and ever would be.

'Well?' he said.

Tala scanned her mind. She felt that she could ask him for anything, about anything. She thought of all the things that she may have wanted in her life, as the years went by, of comforts here and there of which she had been deprived, of all those times that she wished she could have had another life, something other than what she had been given. But now, when it came to it, she realised that she would not change anything at all, for every little thing that she had been through had made her who she was today, every hardship had made her learn. No. Tala did not want to change her life anymore. She wanted to embrace it as fully as possible. To never waste another minute.

'What is my purpose?' she asked, the words coming to her, instinctively almost, and at this, the tortoise merely raised his eyebrows and nodded his head a little.

She said it again, a little louder, and with more conviction:

'What is my purpose?'

And the tortoise just kept on nodding his head.

And all of a sudden she realised that somewhere, deep inside of her, she knew, that she had always known; she had just forgotten that she knew. The tortoise was reflecting the very essence of her being back to her. She became aware of the light around the tortoise; it was expanding, and soon, she too, was in it. Together, they went shooting back up the beam of light on which the tortoise had descended, and she found herself up above the clouds in an ancient library. She turned to look and the tortoise was there – on a throne of sorts – guarding the entrance. This was his home. This was where the knowledge of the universe was stored. All of it.

Tala walked around the library, slowly, respectfully. It appeared to have no end, no walls, no ceilings, just book after book after book, and it was as she was walking thus, that she felt a strong magnetic pull towards her left. She followed the pull, and it got stronger, so strong that she virtually fell into a pile of books. She sat on the ground beside them, and one of them almost spoke to her. It was as if it were saying:

'Me, me, me.'

She picked it up – a large, heavy book, almost the size of her – and brushed aside the dust on the front cover, and there was her name in large golden letters, and a picture of her too: a picture she had not seen, or indeed lived through, and

yet a picture that somehow seemed familiar. She was wearing a garland and carrying a stick. A girl of the forest. It must have been about the age she was now. She opened the front cover and looked inside. Every thought and every feeling that she had ever had, every word that she had ever expressed, every action that she had ever taken, every intent that she had ever had. It was all there. It was a record of her life. She turned to the page she was at that day, and the thoughts that were running through her mind, already they were there. She turned to the future, and it too was there. It was all based on cause and effect: her thoughts, feelings and actions of today affected her reality of tomorrow, affected the quality of what she attracted into her life. She could see it all so clearly.

For a moment, she thought this knowledge was too great to hold, and she tried to block it, and she saw, before her very eyes, her future changing into something so much less than what it could be. She stopped, she reconsidered, and she knew that she was ready to fulfil her destiny, and the future before her brightened like a rising sun.

'You see,' said the tortoise, 'when people try to fight against their purpose, they are never happy, they live a joyless life of mediocrity. You could say, they miss the whole point of life.'

Tala saw a vision of herself leading a group of children through the woods, and she knew, in that instant, what she must do next. She turned to look at the tortoise, and the tortoise sent her the image of a key. Tala knew that she had been accepted, that she had access to this library whenever she chose, that she could use it to help many on their path, for this library held a book for everyone who was now, had ever been and ever would be. Tala could see the truth now. Tala remembered who she was – not just skin and bones as she had been led to believe. She remembered where she came from, what she had been through over many different lifetimes. She had access to it all. She knew that this life – her life – was but a game, an opportunity to develop and learn and grow, a mere trifle in the totality of all that was. She knew that each person on this planet – and beyond – has a unique purpose to fulfil, and she had the key to help them, just as she had been helped. But first of all they must be open to receiving, just as she had been.

'You see,' said the tortoise, 'Tala's purpose was to awaken the human race – no less than that – to help them see through the illusion, to lift the veil from their eyes, just as the veil had been lifted from hers. And what better place to start than with her own kind – children – for children are so much closer to the truth than adults. They have not yet had the chance to become disillusioned with life – or at least not yet completely so.'

Tala looked at the tortoise and nodded. She closed her eyes and she was back in the forest. She lay down on the ground, feeling the earth beneath her, and as she did so, the task before her was laid clear; the steps that she would take to set forth the spiral of events that was to follow crystallised into her view.

XVIII

Everything has got to change. That was the message of Tala's first gathering in the woods.

She had travelled far and wide handpicking fellow children who she knew would be open to the task at hand. These children had not been hard to find, for what united them all was that they stood out from the masses. Their light shone more brightly than most. And as a result of this, they had all met with trouble on their path with those who did not understand them, with those who tried to convince them that they were wrong, with those who tried to impose the narrow confines of their belief system on them because they were afraid of the truth.

'You see,' said the tortoise, 'grown adults would sense something inside of these children that they were not yet ready to receive, and so, as with all tyrants, they tried to stop it, rather than to look at themselves.'

Some of these children had started to believe that they were wrong, and Tala had caught them just in time, before they well and truly went off the rails – *if the world isn't interested in what I have to say, then I might as well misbehave*, was the general attitude – whilst others never doubted for a moment that they were right, and that the so-called voices of authority were wrong.

By now, they were all standing in a circle around a fire – hand in hand – and a beautiful indigo blue colour rose far up into the sky around them. The colour of the third eye – or inner eye – or whatever you like to call it, for these children all had a far-reaching vision; they had the capacity to see things that others could not see. They were all connected to their guides in one way or another, even if they did not quite know it, even if the environment they had been brought up in had spent years telling them that it was make-believe.

Now, here they were, at what Tala had christened 'The Pixikins' School': a place to reconnect with who they really were. There were no rigid rules and regulations here, as with so many other established so-called learning places. No. Here they were free to be themselves. Free to ask the questions that mattered to them. And they did not get into trouble if they disagreed with what they were told. It was a place for them to discover, for themselves, what was true and what brought meaning to their lives, in the way that suited who they were. It was a place that was designed to allow each and every individual to flourish in their very own way, not a breeding ground to create a certain type of person, or a certain type of behaviour. And they could ask whosoever they pleased for guidance, for there were no hierarchies here: Tala, each other, any number of their guides, or the pixikins, for Tala had by now told them her story. And she could be a channel between the pixikins and the other children, helping them connect with each other, until, little by little, some of them learnt to connect by themselves.

'You see,' said the tortoise, 'these children were all born with an inbuilt capacity that was greater than most. They could fathom great truths that grown adults were terrified of. They could sense when they were being lied to, when someone was trying to pull the wool over their eyes, and it filled them with a burning rage, a burning rage to make the world a better place.'

The tortoise paused for dramatic effect, before continuing:

'You could say that they were a fiery bunch, but that is no bad thing when it encourages people to question what they know, inside, is wrong, when it encourages them to go forth and change the world. Yes. These children were all completely and

utterly unique – they knew what they stood for –
but what united them all was their warrior spirit.
I'll say it again, warrior spirit, for that is what these
children were – warriors. These children were
here to fight for justice: justice against those who
tried to harm them, justice against those who tried
to harm others, justice against those who tried
to impose their rigid view on the world. These
children all had a very important life purpose.
These children were here to rock the boat, so to
speak, to pave the way to a brighter future where
all things and all people are treated as equals.'

They continued standing there, holding hands,
and the power of their collective spirits conjured

up an image in the very centre of them – a little like a movie screen. They saw the world as it was then – with war and chaos and destruction all around them – the power being held by the few who made decisions out of fear and greed and a desire to dominate. It did not matter whether it was schools, the workplace, governments or a court of law, for as with all things – good and bad – it starts small, and escalates. Things had got out of control. People were fighting their own kind – for what? Killing their own kind – for what? These people had forgotten that they were all a part of the collective whole: that damaging their neighbour was damaging themselves. These people needed to be stopped, and these children, standing right there, were the ones who were going to stop them.

XIX

'We are the warrior children, and we remember who we are,' the children said, as they entered the school accompanied by their angels, the ascended masters, their spirit animals, the fairies, their spirit guides, and the pixikins, no less.

At first, of course, they were laughed at, ridiculed, as they had come to expect in their lives – the school called security, or, worse, the parents of these children to come and take them away – but little by little, they gathered momentum. The cause grew. The children went from school to school. Other children heard by word of mouth and flocked to join them; other children just like them, and even those who were not quite like them, but saw merit in their cause. Soon, there were so many of them that people had to listen. Meetings were set up between adults and children where the children spoke their truth: told them what was working, what wasn't working and why it wasn't working.

And then there was the big divide: those who were with them, and those who were opposed to them. It was a war of sorts, but not a war that left destruction in its wake. No. It was a subtle war: forces of good against forces of evil. Say, Tala

was having a conversation with Mr Briggs, and
Mr Briggs was trying to assert his authority over
her. Well, it was not just Tala's words that were
having an effect. All manner of activity was going
on behind the scenes, in the other realms. Tala's
guides, together with his guides, were fighting the
demons that had got ahold of him – the demons
that had led him to believe that he was more
important than anyone else. These demons lived in
the lower levels of the universe: the realms where
Tala had not been.

'For, as you need to be vibrating at a higher level
to ascend the realms,' said the tortoise, 'so too, do
you need to be vibrating at a lower level, in order

to descend.'

Now Tala could see everything. She could see where the demons had started to get ahold of people, for they, too, did what they could to gather people to their cause, and the lower people sunk, the more susceptible they were to being preyed upon. In the case of Mr Briggs, he was not too far gone and was still reachable. And so, little by little, the forces of good prevailed over the forces of evil, but this was not always so – not for everyone – and this is why wars start. People descend lower and lower and lower, until they have moved so far from their path, that all they are hungry for is death and destruction.

Little by little, things did start to change, and the children were given more free will at school. Creatively speaking they were allowed to express themselves in whatever manner they chose, rather than having to follow rigid rules and all create the same piece of work. If a child disagreed with what a teacher said, they were no longer sent out of the classroom and told to write lines; instead, a healthy debate was encouraged. People started to understand that sometimes children can and do know more than adults, especially when it comes to what their needs are. Children started to be consulted on decisions that would affect them – so obvious and yet previously not so obvious to the so-called grown-ups. Children who were connected to their guides were no longer ostracised; instead, they were encouraged to build that connection – a connection that would prove very valuable to them throughout their lives.

Tala kept her own training camp going in the forest – especially for children like her: children who were a bit different from the masses. It was a place where they could go and gather strength. A place where they could go and connect with the pixikins and all the guidance they had to offer. A place where they could go and be inspired to keep doing the good work that they were doing. And what started out on a small scale, gradually expanded, from schools, to organisations, to government offices, and to the battlefield. The children fought with words of truth and light, and carried such conviction that, by and by, some adults cottoned on and joined their cause.

'They were a little slower on the uptake, mind you,' said the tortoise, with a smirk on his face, 'but eventually they got there.'

The world was changing all around them. People were waking up. What Tala and her clan did was to lead by example. They became a movement, and the more people who joined them, the more powerful they became; the higher their collective vibration, the more the forces of evil would have to sink away from them with their tails between their legs. Tala did not have to do anything. It was the light atmosphere that hurt their skin. There was no place for them in this new world. And as Tala grew up, she held true to her values, and the next generation of children that followed was purer still; what Tala had done was to pave the way to a new way of being, a new breed of being, and nothing short of that.

'You see,' said the tortoise, 'you may look upon the bad things that happen in the world and think that there is nothing to be done, but in actual fact, each and everyone of us can do our bit. It starts with taking care of ourselves, and treating other people how we would wish to be treated. After all, who would have thought that one little girl accidentally slipping on a banana skin would be enough to change the world?'

XX

Tala was alone in the woods – well, I say alone, but naturally she was surrounded by all manner of guides and pixikins, and well-wishers on her path. What I mean to say, is that she was alone on the earthly plane. She was sleeping out under the stars, as was her way. A habit she had picked up way back when, as she had traversed the layers of the universe with Rollo by her side. She felt a little nudge and quietly opened her eyes. There was no one to be seen – perhaps she had imagined it – but something compelled her to sit up, and as she did, she saw the silhouette of a figure up ahead in the distance between the trees.

'Tala,' she heard through the sound of the wind.

And there was nothing that could have kept her away. Her soul was calling her, compelling her to move forward. She moved towards the figure quietly, and with trepidation. It was an American Indian wearing a full headdress. She did not know if he was human or spirit, but it was all the same to her. He smiled at her and then turned his back and started walking, and Tala followed suit. They walked together in silence, effortlessly crossing all manner of different landscapes: mountains, icebergs, rain forests, deserts. Tala felt the icy cold, the humidity, the sweltering heat. She saw the wildlife that accompanied each landscape. And suddenly, Tala understood that it was all a metaphor for life. Tala could walk through all terrains now, meet with any peril, for she had developed inside of her a self-sufficiency: an inner core.

By now, they were out in the middle of the desert – a wide, open expanse of land – and the American Indian stopped and built a fire. Tala stood there watching the fire as it grew, and she realised that it, too, was a metaphor for the fire that was burning within her, the fire that signified

her passion for life, the fire that would compel her to keep moving forwards in her very own special way, no matter what anyone said. They stood up and kept going on their journey. Tala did not know where they were going, but she knew, without a shadow of a doubt, that she was heading in the right direction, and for that she was grateful.

35805354R00074

Printed in Great Britain
by Amazon